ONE WARM FOX

NICK BUTTERWORTH

TED SMART

"Shoo! Go on, shoo!" said Percy the park keeper. "This isn't bird seed. Shoo!"

Percy was sowing some wild flower seed on a patch of bare earth. But a bunch of rooks who had suddenly appeared were trying to gobble up the seed as fast as Percy could scatter it.

"And you're not much help," said Percy to a rather saggy-looking scarecrow he had made. He sighed and tried to cover the last of the seed with his rake.

When Percy got back to his hut,
he found his friend the fox sitting
on the steps. Next to the fox there was
a parcel.

"Hello," said Percy. "I see
the postman has been."

Percy picked up the parcel and looked at the writing.

"Oh dear," he said.

"What's the matter?" said the fox. "Don't you like parcels?"

"Not from Auntie Joyce," said Percy. "She knits things. This will be another pullover or a scarf or something. I've got a collection."

Percy began to open the parcel.
"She's very kind," said Percy, "but
somehow, the things she knits. . .well,
they don't really suit me. Not my sort
of colours. Either that or they don't fit."

"**P**erhaps they'd fit me," said the fox.
"I was a bit chilly last night."
Percy unwrapped the rest of the parcel.

"Well, this will keep your ears warm,"
he chuckled, and he tossed the fox a
woolly balaclava. "Very nice, but a bit
small for me, I think."

The fox pulled on the balaclava.
He looked a bit disappointed.
"I was thinking more of a pullover,"
he said. "This is squashing my ears."

Percy smiled.
      "Follow me," he said.
  "Pardon?" said the fox.

"I said follow me," Percy repeated
loudly, and he led the fox into his hut.

Percy brought out an old suitcase from under his bed. He blew the dust off it and opened it.

"How about this?" Percy held up one of Auntie Joyce's pullovers. The fox put it on.

"It fits!" said the fox happily.

"So it does," said Percy with a chuckle. "In that case, help yourself. I'm just going to check my wild flower patch."

Percy wasn't gone for long. As he walked back towards his hut, he didn't look too pleased.

B ut, as soon as Percy opened the door, his face changed.

"Everything fits!" said the fox.
Percy roared with laughter.

"You can't go about like that!" he said.
"Anyway, you'll be much too hot. You'll cook!"

"It is a bit warm," admitted the fox. "I just thought, at night, you know. . ."

"You can keep the pullover," said Percy, "but I think you should take off the rest. Besides, I think I know someone that these things might suit."

The next morning, Percy was out working in the park when he met the fox again.

"How were you last night?" asked Percy.

"As warm as toast!" said the fox. "How is your wild flower patch? Are those rooks still being a nuisance?"

"I can't understand it," Percy chuckled.
"They haven't been near the place!"

NICK BUTTERWORTH

Nick Butterworth was born in North London in 1946 and grew up in a sweet shop in Essex. He now lives in Suffolk with his wife Annette and their two children, Ben and Amanda.

The inspiration for the Percy the Park Keeper books came from Nick Butterworth's many walks through the local park with the family dog, Jake. The stories have now been made into a stunning animated television series, available on video from HIT Entertainment plc.